Text copyright © 1992 by Hiawyn Oram
Illustrations copyright © 1992 by Tony Ross

Published by Crown Publishers, Inc., a Random House company,
225 Park Avenue South, New York, New York 10003
First published in Great Britain in 1992 by Andersen Press Ltd.
Published in Australia by Random Century Australia Pty., Ltd.
CROWN is a trademark of Crown Publishers, Inc.

Manufactured in Scotland

Library of Congress Cataloging-in-Publication Data
Oram, Hiawyn.
Reckless Ruby / Hiawyn Oram ; illustrated by Tony Ross.
p.   cm.
Summary: To change her parents' minds about how "precious" she is, Ruby
performs more and more wildly reckless feats, from diving off roofs into
fishbowls to hanging from skyscrapers by her shoelaces.
[1. Parent and child—Fiction.   2. Behavior—Fiction.]   I. Ross,
Tony, ill.   II. Title.
PZ7.0624Re   1992
[E]—dc20   91-20124
ISBN 0-517-58744-0

10 9 8 7 6 5 4 3 2 1
First American Edition

Reckless Ruby

by Hiawyn Oram
illustrated by Tony Ross

CROWN PUBLISHERS, INC.

New York

Once there was a little girl called Ruby. Ruby glowed like the jewel she was named after. People couldn't help noticing.

"Ruby is so beautiful!" they said. "Ruby is so precious!"

"Don't I know it!" said her mother. "Ruby is so precious
I call her 'Precious.' Ruby is so precious I expect she'll grow
up and marry a prince who'll wrap her in cotton and only
bring her out for glittering banquets."

Ruby tried hard not to hear these dreadful predictions about her future. But they were made so often she couldn't help it, and she went to see her friend Harvey for advice.

"You could try not being precious," said Harvey.

"But how?" said Ruby.

"By getting reckless," said Harvey.

So Ruby got reckless. Very, very reckless. She got so reckless she told all the children on the playground that she could fly . . .

. . . and had four stitches in her head because she couldn't.

"Oh, Ruby! Precious baby!" wailed her mother. "If you
don't take better care of yourself, you're never going to grow
up to marry a prince and get wrapped in cotton and only
come out for glittering banquets."

"GOOD!" thought Ruby . . .

. . . and got more reckless and said she could dance like a
Russian acrobat on the bars of a moving bicycle . . .

. . . and had another four stitches in her head because she couldn't.

"Oh, Ruby! Rubikins!" said her granny. "Eight stitches and not even seven years old! If you don't take better care of yourself, you are never going to grow up to marry a prince and get wrapped in cotton and only come out to give the servants orders."

"GREAT!" thought Ruby . . .

    ... and grew more reckless and ran away to sea and when
the ship's captain found her, she told him her father was
really an ogre in a pin-striped suit and her mother was a
she-wolf in stone-washed jeans and on no account should he
send her home or they'd eat her up ...

. . . which caused Ruby's father to come home early from the office and get very, very angry.

"Ruby, this will not do," he said. "If you do not stop lying and start taking better care of yourself, you will never grow up to marry a prince, which will be very, very disappointing for your mother and me."

"Sorry," said Ruby, lying again . . .

. . . and grew so reckless she said she could dive off any roof into a fishbowl . . .

. . . and dangle from skyscrapers by her shoelaces . . .

. . . and walk on water in lead boots . . .

. . . and cross canyons single-handed . . .

. . . and eat fire,
and swords,
and porcupines . . .

. . . and climb into a python's cage
and shake hands with an octopus . . .

. . . and smoke five cigars in the shrubbery without feeling
sick . . .

   . . . and spent six weeks in the hospital because she couldn't. Or not without two broken legs, two black eyes, five fractured ribs, sixteen stitches, ten broken fingers, eight purple bruises, and a very, very funny feeling in her stomach.

When her mother and father came to visit her, they were
not very pleased.

"You are a very, very reckless little girl," they said.

"Not precious?" said Ruby.

"Not precious at all!" cried her mother.

"Not precious one bit?" said Ruby.

"Not precious one tiny, little bit!" snapped her father.

"Not precious enough to grow up to marry a prince and be wrapped in cotton and only come out for glittering banquets and to tell the servants what to do?"

"Certainly not!" wept her mother.

"Never!" wailed her father.

"WHEW!" said Ruby . . .

. . . and got better immediately and went to see Harvey.
"It's all OK, Harv. I can stop being reckless and grow up."
"And marry me?" said Harvey hopefully.

"And be a firefighter," said Ruby happily.